Today I Feel Silly
& Other MOODS That Make My Day

by Jamie Lee Curtis

illustrated by Laura Cornell

Joanna Cotler Books
An Imprint of HarperCollins*Publishers*

Thanks to the three "moodsketeers"—
Joanna, Phyllis and Laura.
And special thanks to Annie, for fixing the end.

Today I Feel Silly & Other Moods That Make My Day

http://www.harperchildrens.com Library of Congress Cataloging-in-Publication Data Curtis, Jamie Lee, date.
Today I feel silly & other moods that make my day / Jamie Lee Curtis ; illustrated by Laura Cornell.
p. cm. "Joanna Cotler books." Summary: A child's emotions range from silliness to anger to excitement, coloring and changing each day.
ISBN 0-06-024560-3 [1. Emotions—Fiction. 2. Stories in rhyme.] I. Cornell, Laura, ill. II. Title.
PZ7.3.C9344To 1998 97-31416 [E]—dc21 CIP AC Designed by Alicia Mikles Paper engineering by Gene Vosough
16 17 18 19 20 ❖

To my sister, Kelly,
who reminds me to do my smile exercises every day.
–J.L.C.

To Glenna
–L.C.

kit
FOX
BOX

Today I feel silly.
Mom says it's the heat.
I put rouge on the cat
and gloves on my feet.
I ate noodles for breakfast
and pancakes at night.
I dressed like a star
and was quite a sight.

SPY KIT
CAPE
ALL KINDS of Capes
ALL ABOUT ELVES
ALL ABOUT ELVES
ORIGAMI
5 in 1 Dance Kit
HULA FOXTROT
TWIST CHA CHA
BOX O' STEPS
Meet MR. OTTER
The Hula

Today my mood's bad. I feel grumpy and mean.
I picked up my room. It still isn't clean.
I forgot to feed Franny and water the fern.
And the cocoa I'm making is starting to burn.

Today I am angry. You'd better stay clear.
My face is all pinched and red ear to ear.

My friends had a play date. They left me out.
My feelings are hurt. I want to shout!

Today I am joyful. My mood is first-rate.
My friend's sleeping over, she said she can't wait.
My freckles are popping, the sun is so bright.
I ran in the relay with all of my might.

BABY SWING
SCARY SLIDE
MOOD SWING
HYPERACTIVE STRAIGHT-A-WAY

Today I'm confused, my life's getting hairy.
Sam says he's my boyfriend but he also likes Mary.
My mom told my father he might be a dad.
I might get a brother. I'm not sure I'm glad.

Today I am quiet, my mom understands.
She gave me two ice creams and then we held hands.

We went to the movies and then had a bite.
I cried just a little and then felt all right.

Today I'm excited there's so much to do.
I'm going to sell cookies and lemonade too.

I'm starting a club to go clean up the park.

And I've got a big crush on my teacher named Mark.

Today I am cranky
so nothing seems right.
I have diarrhea
and broke my new kite.

Mom dyed her hair orange.

My dad shaved his beard.

My tooth came in crooked.
This family is weird.

Lilac Fairy
YELLOW

Today I am lonely. I feel so small.
My Auntie's *away*. I wish that she'd call.
My mom's working late and my dad has the flu.
And although I've got stuff I've got nothing to do.

Today I am happy. I'm walking on air.

I learned how to knit

and to French-braid my hair.

I did my first solo in hip-hop and jazz.

This day's been so great, I am full of pizzazz.

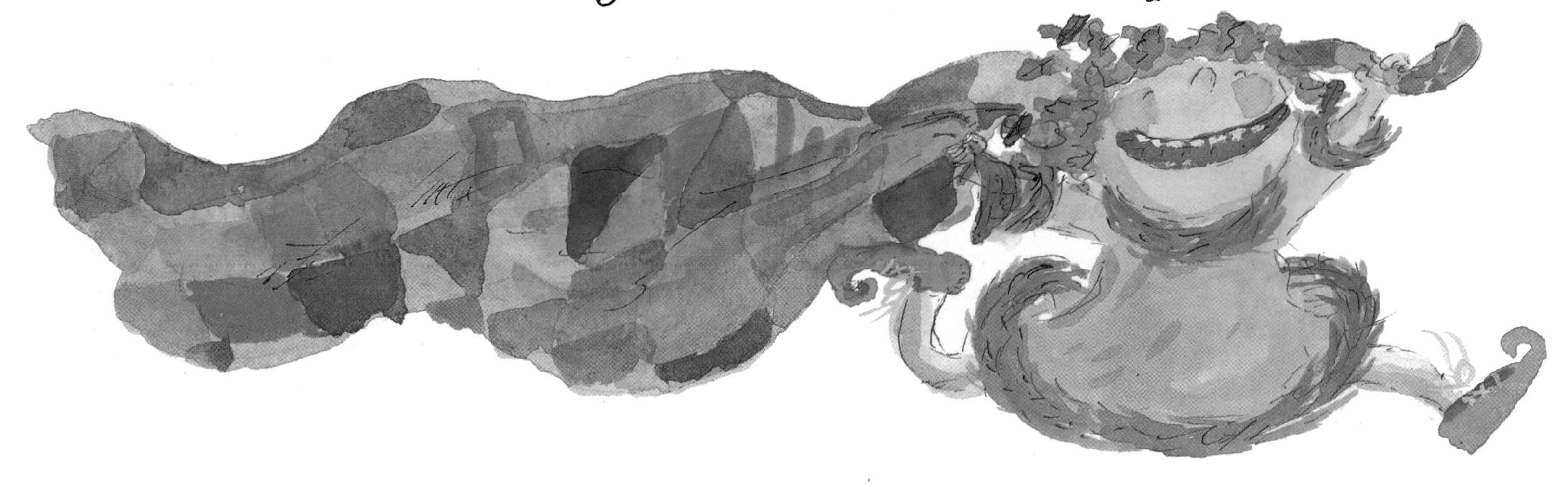

Star Sleek
STRAIGHT HAIR SALVE
Ever So Young
EYE GEL

Today I'm discouraged and frustrated—see?
I tried Rollerblading and fell on my knee.
I really want straight hair,
but mine's curly-q.
Should I cut it or grow it,
oh what should I do?

Today I am sad, my mood's heavy and gray.
There's a frown on my face and it's been there all day.
My best friend and I had a really big fight.
She said that I tattled and I know that she's right.

Today my mood's great, it's the absolute best.
I rode a two-wheeler and passed my math test.
I played soccer at recess and we won the game.
I sang in the show and my parents both came.

I'd rather feel silly, excited or glad,
than cranky or grumpy, discouraged or sad.
But moods are just something that happen each day.
Whatever I'm feeling inside is okay!

The Hula

How do YOU
feel today? . . .